# The Father Christmas Trap

## Margaret Stonborough and Sarah Lenton

## Young Lions

# For Christopher and Andrew.

Published in Young Lions 1989
8 Grafton Street, London W1X 3LA

Young Lions is an imprint of
the Children's Division, part of
the Collins Publishing Group

Printed in Great Britain by
William Collins Sons & Co. Ltd, Glasgow

It was Christmas Eve, and the children,

Andrew

Christopher

and Sarah,

were getting ready for Father Christmas. Sarah was writing a last minute letter to him, '. . . a f-u-t-b-a-l-l, a s-p-a-c h-e-l-m-e-t, a p-e-d-a-l c-a-r . . .', she spelt out.

3

'All our socks are too small,' said Christopher, 'the presents will never fit in!'

'We need something bigger,' said Sarah, looking up from her letter. 'I know – Daddy's sailor socks.'

'I'll get them!'
said Christopher.

He was back

in a flash.

5

he said, gleefully dropping them on the floor.

'Children!' Mummy called up the stairs, 'are you ready to post the letter yet?'
'Just a minute!' Sarah shouted back, signing her name at the bottom.

'Oh help, I haven't stuck up my stocking yet.'

Andrew gave her a hand.

'Where shall we hide the toys?'
asked Christopher.

Hey.

'Under the bed?'

'Yes, and some
can go in the
doll's pram,'
said Sarah.

CLONK!

'We're ready!' called Christopher to
Mummy downstairs,
and took a
flying
leap
into his
bed.

Wheeee

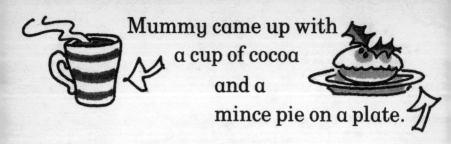

Mummy came up with a cup of cocoa and a mince pie on a plate.

'These are for Father Christmas when he comes,' she said and put them down on the bedside table.
'Now where is this letter for Father Christmas?

A futball?

I hope Father Christmas can understand this!'

Does it need another 'f'?

The fire in the playroom grate had
died right down, and there was only
a wisp of warm smoke rising up
the chimney.

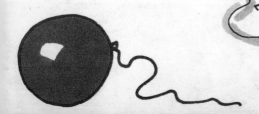

ZZZZZZRRRMMM

'The letter won't burn, will it?' asked Sarah, anxiously.

'No, there's only just enough heat left to carry the letter up the chimney,' said Mummy as she unhooked the fire-guard and held the letter over the smoke.

'Everybody into bed,' she said
and tucked them up
carefully, each in turn.
'Remember, Father
Christmas won't come
unless you are very good
and go to sleep at once.'
And with that she switched off the
light and went out.

Little Andrew fell asleep at once.

'Father
Christmas
will come
tonight,
won't he?'

'Yes, but
you have to
be asleep.'

'Sarah, where does Father Christmas live?'

F. CHRISTMAS
BEWARE of THE REINDEER

'In Greenland. Now go to sleep.'

16

'Sarah, if he lives in Greenland, how does he get here, then?'

He flies through the night on a sledge drawn by reindeer.

'And does he bring presents to all the children in the world?'

17

'Then he just gives them a lump of
coal. Now go to sleep.'

'Sarah!'

'Sshht!'

'Sarah,' said Christopher, 'will Father Christmas see his cocoa and mince pie in the dark?'

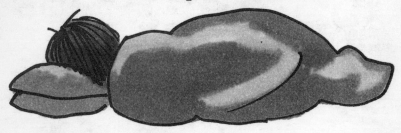

'Yes, of course. Now go to . . .'
'Sarah — even the holly?'

'Oh no. We'd better take it off,' said Sarah, stretching an arm out of bed and flinging

FLING

watch this

the holly

Wheee

on the floor . . .

Wheeee

where . . .

it landed on a stray balloon. . .

uh,oh

21

The three children were suddenly
very wide awake.

'What happened?' said Christopher, putting on the light.

CLICK

'I think the holly must have touched a balloon,' said Sarah. 'Do put out the light and go to sleep or he won't come, you know.'

But I want to see Father Christmas

'Well you can't,'
said Sarah.

'But Sarah, supposing . . .
supposing I
*accidentally* woke up
when he came –
that wouldn't be my fault,
would it?'

'No, but – Christopher!
– what are you doing?'

'I'm just putting
the skate-board
by the grate.'

'Christopher, you can't do that!' said Sarah, horrified.
'Father Christmas might step on it and . . .'

*Oh . . . . . dear*

'That's the point!' said Christopher, carefully arranging a drum opposite the skate-board.

Let's use Andrew's panda to see if it works.

SHOVE

Christopher pushed the panda as far up the chimney as he could, and let go.

Nothing happened. The panda was stuck.

He gave it a sharp tug — the panda

cough....

WHOOOSHED down in a shower of soot

26

. . . landed on the skate-board,

skidded

across the floor,
and . . :

. . . crashed

into a lorry.

'That won't work,' said Christopher, scratching his head.

Andrew climbed out of his cot

and rescued his sooty panda.

He got back into
his cot and dialled
Father Christmas on
his toy telephone.

'Don't . . . don't . . . don't . . .' he tried
to warn Father Christmas, but
there was no answer.

'Ssshht!' said Sarah and Christopher
together. 'Or Mummy will hear you.'

'You know,'
said Sarah,
getting caught up
in the idea.
'We could tie Andrew's rattle
to the handle
of the
cocoa mug,

and then tie the rattle to the drawer.

Then – look – I'll pretend to be
Father Christmas: I come in with
my sack of toys . . .

... eat it ...

... then I pick up the cocoa,'

The cocoa

spilt

everywhere.

'It was cold anyway,' said Sarah.

34

The children sat on her bed,
deep in thought.

Sarah dabbed
at the spilt cocoa with her duvet cover.

'What shall we do about the cocoa?'
asked Christopher. He looked around
the room.

'Sarah, your painting-water is
almost the colour of cocoa. Let's
just add some more brown paint and . .'

EMPTY

'Don't touch,' said Sarah, licking her paintbrush. 'I'll do this myself.'

Soon she had just the right colour.

'I'll make a mince pie out of the plasticine,' said Christopher.

'Don't be silly,' said Sarah, 'it's blue.'

She put the pretend cocoa back
on the bedside table. Christopher
undid the string.

'If only we had enough string,' he
said, 'we could make a tiger trap
to catch Father Christmas.'

'A tiger trap? Of course!'
said Sarah. 'And we can use the
cocoa as the bait. But we'll never
find enough string.'

'Oh yes we will,' said Christopher. 'Look, there's Andrew's train,

your kite,

my shoe laces . . .'

'No Andrew, don't pull that!'
they said together.

'Look Sarah, we could use these balloon strings too – well done Andrew!' said Christopher.

Well, they're not having my tail.

They set to work in silence, undoing
every piece of string they could
find, untying every knot and then
joining all the pieces up into one
enormous long length.

'Now,' said Christopher, 'for the tiger trap.'

He carefully tied one end of the string to the leg at the bottom of his bed.

Then he gave the string to Sarah.

She tied the string to the leg at
the head of her bed.

Tell me
when it's
safe to come
out

Sarah passed the string back to
Christopher and so they worked on
in silence, until it
looked like this.

The children looked at their handiwork.

'It's the best tiger trap we've ever made,' said Christopher, yawning.

'No,' said Sarah, who was beginning to feel very sleepy indeed, 'it's not a tiger trap, it's a *Father Christmas Trap*! Let's go to sleep now and we will wake up when he's caught.'

They put Andrew back into his cot . . .

switched out
the light,
and went back to bed.

'Goodnight,' they said . . .

. . . and there was silence.

In the middle of the night . . .

. . . something shook Sarah's bed.

It happened again.

Sarah and Christopher woke up
with a start.

What was that?

It was very dark in the room.
A deep bass voice spoke,

Drat! There's string
all over the deck and I am
caught in it!

'Help!' thought Christopher and
Sarah,

We've caught
FATHER CHRISTMAS!

And dived down their beds.

Christopher risked a peep.

Horror!

A large black figure
was standing by his bed.

'Put the light on, darling,' said
the voice. The light went on.

cried Andrew joyfully.

Sarah and Christopher sat up quickly.

'We thought you were
Father Christmas,' said Christopher.
'What's all this string for?' asked
Daddy, trying to untangle himself.
'It's not string,' said Christopher,
'it's a Father Christmas Trap!'

'Come and help me clear it away.
Thank heavens I came up to make sure
everything was ship-shape,'
said Daddy.

Mummy went to get some more hot
cocoa from the kitchen.

Sarah and Christopher removed the string. Daddy straightened their beds and tucked them in again, firmly.

Mummy came back with the cocoa and another mince pie.

'Daddy,' said Christopher, 'Daddy, would Father Christmas have been very cross?'

'Yes,' said Daddy, 'very cross! Now go to sleep and no more nonsense. Good night.'

'Good night,' said the children.

Daddy switched off the light and went out. All was still.

Next morning Sarah woke up first.
She turned over in bed. Something
heavy and rustly lay across her feet.
She sat up quickly to look.

'Christopher,' she cried, 'wake up!
Father Christmas has been – the
stockings are *full* . . . and look . . .

the mug is EMPTY!'

**THE END**